Mariana and Her Familia

By **MÓNICA MANCILLAS**   Illustrated by **ERIKA MEZA**

BALZER + BRAY
An Imprint of HarperCollinsPublishers

Mariana's tummy did a little flip as she and Mami drove across the frontera. México was a jumble of mismatched buildings of all shapes and sizes. The noisy streets were full of the rhythms of mariachi and singsongy vendors. The air smelled of gasoline and fish, and even the radio spoke Spanish.

"This was your first home," Mami said as they arrived at Abuelita's house. But Mariana did not feel at home. Abuelita's house was a stranger.

"¡Pásense! Pásense!" Abuelita said as she waved Mariana inside. She gave Mariana a warm welcome hug and a cheekful of grandma kisses.

Mariana and Mami walked to the sala, where the whole familia was waiting. At home, there was only Mariana and Mami. But here, there was lots of family.

There was Tía Luz and Tío Juan, Prima Sara and Primo Ernesto, Tía Rebecca and Tío Hernan, and other people too. Mariana recognized most of their faces from pictures she had seen back home.

But she still felt shy as she looked around at this house filled with brand-new people.

Mariana sat with her tíos and Mami as they talked to each other in Spanish. She understood a few of the words, but she only knew how to say "gracias." She watched as Prima Sara tagged Primo Ernesto and yelled, "La Traes!" It looked like fun to play tag, but she was too afraid to join in.

"Why don't you hand out the presents we brought?"
Mami gently suggested. Mariana smiled as she suddenly
remembered the gifts they had brought from home.

She gave her tíos a tin of cookies and a bag
of fancy chocolates. Her primos grinned as they
unwrapped the toys Mariana had picked out.

Mariana saved the best for last.

"This one is for agualita." Mariana blushed
as all of her tíos and primos began to giggle.

"It's *abuelita*," Mami said.
"Oh," Mariana whispered.
Mariana was so embarrassed, she wished that she could hide.

"Ven aquí, Chiquita." Abuelita beckoned Mariana to follow.

Mariana's eyes went wide as she saw what Abuelita was holding.
"A book!" she said.
"Un libro."
"Un libro," Mariana repeated.
Mariana had read this story before, but *this* book was in Spanish.

Mariana smiled as she opened the book
and looked at the colorful pictures.
  "This is the Big Bad Wolf," she said.

"*Un Lobo*," Abuelita said.

"Un lobo,"
Mariana repeated.

"*Un Lobo Hambriento*,"
Abuelita growled.

Mariana squealed as the hungry wolf
chased after the three cochinitos.

When they were done reading, Mariana put a hand to her empty belly.

"Hambre," she said. Abuelita smiled and walked Mariana to the kitchen.

Abuelita warmed the tortillas while Mariana pulled the cheese.

"Queso," Abuelita said.

"Queso," Mariana repeated.

Mariana helped Abuelita sprinkle the queso on the tortillas. Her primos followed the tempting smell of crispy quesadillas.

Prima Sara helped to mash the beans into creamy, rich frijoles while Mami stirred the arroz and Primo Ernesto husked the elotes. Together, they set the table and filled the glasses with limonada. At home, Mami made lunch by herself. But here, lunch was a party.

Later, while dinner was cooking, Abuelita sat down to rest and open her present.

"It's a picture!" Mariana said.

"Una fotografía," said Abuelita.

"Where should we put it?" Mariana asked.

"Aquí," said Abuelita.

She showed Mariana a special wall filled with family pictures.

Mariana found the perfect
spot to hang Abuelita's present.

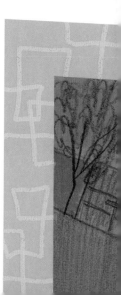

"Now I'm part of the family," she said.

"You always were," said Mami. Mami pointed to a pink-framed picture on the wall.

"Who's that?" Mariana wondered.

"That's you when you were a baby," said Mami.

Mariana looked at the picture next to hers. "Is that me too?" she asked.

"That one is *Agua*lita," said Mami. "She looked a lot like you."

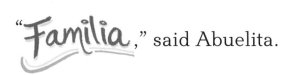

"It's *Abuelita*." Mariana laughed.

"*Familia*," said Abuelita.

Balzer + Bray is an imprint of HarperCollins Publishers.

Mariana and Her Familia
Text copyright © 2022 by Mónica Mancillas
Illustrations copyright © 2022 by Erika Meza
All rights reserved. Manufactured in Italy.

Library of Congress Control Number: 2021939621
ISBN 978-0-06-296246-1

The artist used watercolor pencils, gouache, and childhood memories to create the illustrations for this book.
Typography by Dana Fritts
Hand lettering by Alexandra Snowdon and Erika Meza
22 23 24 25 26 RTLO 10 9 8 7 6 5 4 3 2 1
❖
First Edition